Legacy Untamed: A Forgotten Legacy Novel

A Forgotten Legacy, Volume 1

Marquise The Coach

Published by Marquise The Coach, 2024.

This is a work of fiction. Similarities to real people, places, or events are entirely coincidental.

LEGACY UNTAMED: A FORGOTTEN LEGACY NOVEL

First edition. April 27, 2024.

ISBN: 979-8224563258

Written by Marquise The Coach.

Also by Marquise The Coach

A Forgotten Legacy
Legacy Untamed: A Forgotten Legacy Novel

Standalone
Mind Matters: Nurturing Mental Health and 20 Ways to Improve It
The Forgotten Melody

Watch for more at https://marquisethecoach.com/.

Table of Contents

In a world where whispers of forgotten magic echo through crumbling ruins, a young woman named Lyra stumbles upon a hidden truth.

Legacy Untamed, the thrilling first chapter of the **Forgotten Legacy** series, awaits. Will you join Lyra as she uncovers a power that could rewrite destiny itself?

Chapter 1: Discordant Melody

Lyra's fingers danced across the violin strings, her bow a blur of defiance against the monotonous drone emanating from the central projector.

The sterile white walls of the Corvus Corporation's audition hall mocked her vibrant crimson dress and the fiery passion she poured into her music.

This wasn't art; it was a sterile imitation, a symphony of obedience played note by lifeless note.

Frustration gnawed at her.

For years, she'd dreamt of becoming a prominent composer, her music a beacon of originality and emotion.

But Corvus, the omnipresent corporation that choked the galaxy with its suffocating control, had other plans.

Their "approved" music was a vapid concoction designed to pacify, not inspire.

As the final note of her piece faded, an oppressive silence filled the room.

The three Corvus judges, their faces as unwrinkled and emotionless as the white walls, exchanged glances.

Finally, the head judge, a gaunt woman with eyes like polished obsidian, spoke.

"Your technique is adequate, Lyra," she said, her voice devoid of warmth, "but the composition... it lacks the necessary... pleasantness."

Pleasantness.

That was their buzzword, their euphemism for the bland, emotionless drivel they forced upon the populace.

Lyra suppressed a surge of anger. "Music isn't about pleasantness," she dared to say, her voice shaking slightly, "it's about evoking emotions, telling stories."

The judges' expressions hardened.

"Emotions," the head judge sneered, "are a source of instability, Ms. Vance.

Corvus-approved music fosters harmony, not discord."

Lyra's heart pounded.

Harmony?

It was more like a monotonous dirge designed to lull the masses into a compliant stupor.

"There's more to music than that," she insisted, her voice gaining strength. "There's passion, there's pain, there's..."

The head judge slammed her hand on the table.

"Dismissed!"

Lyra stormed out of the hall, her frustration boiling over.

Every audition was the same – her music, deemed "too expressive," was rejected, leaving her dreams further out of reach.

Back in her cramped apartment, she tossed her violin case onto the worn couch, a bitter sigh escaping her lips.

Just as despair threatened to consume her, a glint of light caught her eye.

Her grandmother's violin case, a simple wooden box she'd inherited, sat on a dusty shelf.

A pang of longing pierced her – her grandmother, a renowned violinist before Corvus' iron grip took hold, had fostered Lyra's love for music.

As Lyra reached for the case, a hidden latch clicked open, revealing a small, velvet-lined compartment.

Inside lay a single, aged sheet of music, its edges tinged with a faint yellow.

A faded inscription on the top caught her breath: "Fragment – Symphony of Defiance – David Berger."

Her heart hammered in her chest. David Berger, a legendary composer whose music had been deemed subversive and subsequently outlawed by Corvus decades ago.

Could this be a fragment of his lost masterpiece?

A thrill of excitement coursed through her, momentarily eclipsing her frustration.

This wasn't just a piece of music; it was a rebellion in a single sheet.

A spark of defiance flickered to life within her. In a world choked by "pleasantness," Lyra had stumbled upon a discordant melody, a challenge to the suffocating control of Corvus.

This was more than just a composition; it was a key, a gateway to a forgotten legacy, and perhaps, the key to her own artistic freedom.

Chapter 2: Shadows and Secrets

LYRA'S APARTMENT BUZZED with nervous energy.

The aged sheet music lay spread on her coffee table, its faded notes whispering of a bygone era.

The inscription, "Fragment – Symphony of Defiance – David Berger," taunted her with its promise and danger.

David Berger, a name that echoed in hushed tones, was a symbol of artistic rebellion crushed by the iron fist of Corvus.

Possessing his music, even a fragment, was akin to holding a ticking time bomb.

Her heart pounded a frantic rhythm as she traced the delicate script.

The fragment, beautiful yet incomplete, hinted at a powerful melody, its emotion raw and unfettered.

It ignited a yearning within her, a yearning for a world where art wasn't a tool for control, but a conduit for the human spirit.

Suddenly, a flicker of movement outside her window sent a jolt of fear through her.

Had she been followed?

She tiptoed to the window, her breath catching in her throat.

A lone figure cloaked in shadow darted across the dimly lit alleyway, disappearing into the labyrinthine streets below.

Suspicion gnawed at her.

Perhaps it was just a stray scavenger, but the timing was unsettling.

Could Corvus be aware of her discovery?

Fear warred with curiosity.

This music was too important to discard, yet holding onto it was a dangerous gamble.

Determined to learn more, she carefully folded the fragment and tucked it away in a hidden compartment within her violin case.

Her grandmother, blessed with foresight, had installed the compartment, perhaps anticipating a time when art would be contraband.

The next morning, Lyra sought out Dr. Anya Sharma, a renowned scholar with a reputation for defying Corvus' cultural restrictions.

Finding her secluded apartment was no easy feat, requiring a network of trusted contacts and a series of coded messages.

Finally, after navigating a maze of back alleys and darkened storefronts, Lyra stood before a weathered door.

A nervous cough escaped her lips as a wizened woman with eyes that held the wisdom of ages opened the door.

"Lyra Vance, I presume," Dr. Sharma said, her voice surprisingly strong for her age. "I've been expecting you."

Lyra's surprise mirrored in Dr. Sharma's smile. "How did you..." she began, then stopped.

This woman held secrets, that much was clear.

"The whispers of rebellion travel far, child," Dr. Sharma said, ushering her inside.

The air inside the apartment hung heavy with the scent of old paper and forgotten lore.

Stacked shelves overflowed with books, their worn spines hinting at stories waiting to be rediscovered.

Lyra explained her discovery, her voice trembling slightly.

Dr. Sharma listened intently, her eyes gleaming with a mix of curiosity and concern.

"The Symphony of Defiance," she murmured, the weight of the name settling heavily on the room.

"You possess a dangerous relic, child," Dr. Sharma said, her voice grave.

"Corvus would stop at nothing to reclaim it." A flicker of fear danced in Lyra's stomach. But the fire for truth and rebellion burned brighter.

"Tell me everything you know," she pleaded, a newfound determination hardening her voice.

Dr. Sharma's lips curved into a knowing smile.

The symphony's secrets were about to be unraveled, but the path ahead would be fraught with danger.

Chapter 3: Echoes in the Dust

———

DR. SHARMA'S VOICE, raspy with age, weaved a tapestry of rebellion and sacrifice.

The Symphony of Defiance, composed by the enigmatic David Berger, was a rallying cry against Corvus' oppressive control over artistic expression.

Its raw melody, filled with defiance and sorrow, had ignited a rebellion decades ago.

Corvus, wielding its iron fist, had ruthlessly suppressed the symphony, labeling it a weapon of sedition.

Berger and his music vanished, becoming a whispered legend among those who yearned for artistic freedom.

Now, with the fragment clutched in her hand, Lyra held a piece of that lost legacy.

"They say the symphony was separated," Dr. Sharma explained, her eyes reflecting the dim light filtering through dusty windows.

"Each fragment scattered across the galaxy, guarded by those who defied Corvus' control."

Fear mingled with excitement within Lyra.

This wasn't just a single piece of music; it was a puzzle, a map leading to a forbidden masterpiece.

But finding the other fragments meant venturing into the shadowy corners of the galaxy, places where Corvus' reach was absolute.

"It's too dangerous," Dr. Sharma said, her voice laced with concern.

"Corvus hunts down anyone suspected of harboring these fragments."

Lyra understood the risk.

Yet, the thought of letting the symphony remain buried in obscurity sparked defiance within her.

"The music... it has power," she insisted, her voice firm. "It can inspire change."

Dr. Sharma's gaze softened.

She saw a flicker of the same fire that had once burned in the hearts of Berger and his supporters.

"Perhaps," she conceded, her voice a sigh.

"But without help, you'll be lost."

And that's when Dr. Sharma mentioned the Scavengers Guild, a loose network of smugglers and information brokers who operated on the fringes of Corvus' control.

They were outcasts, yes, but some, whispered Dr. Sharma, harbored a deep resentment for Corvus' stifling grip.

Following Dr. Sharma's cryptic instructions, Lyra ventured into the underbelly of the city.

Flickering neon signs cast garish shadows on crumbling buildings.

The air was thick with the stench of garbage and desperation. Here, in this cesspool of society, thrived the Scavengers Guild.

She navigated a maze of darkened alleys, finally arriving at a dimly lit bar reeking of stale alcohol and cheap thrills.

A hulking figure with a shaved head and a cybernetic eye stood guard at the entrance.

Lyra showed him the symbol Dr. Sharma had provided - a stylized violin etched on a piece of worn metal.

The guard's expression remained unreadable.

"Tell Jax," he rumbled, his voice like gravel rubbing against metal, "you have information about the Symphony of Defiance."

Lyra's heart pounded with a mix of anticipation and fear.

This was the point of no return.

Stepping inside the bar, she found herself plunged into a cacophony of shouts, drunken laughter, and the pulsating rhythm of off-key music.

Through the haze of smoke and bodies, she spotted her contact – Jax.

He sat hunched over a table, a lone figure shrouded in darkness.

He looked up, revealing a face etched with scars and a haunted look in his eyes.

But it was his cybernetic eye, flickering with an unnerving red glow, that sent a shiver down Lyra's spine.

"Information," he rasped, his voice a low growl.

"Let's hear it."

Lyra, her resolve hardening, took a seat opposite him, ready to reveal the secret that could change everything.

But as she began to speak, a sudden commotion shattered the tense atmosphere.

A group of burly figures, their uniforms emblazoned with the Corvus insignia, pushed their way into the bar.

Lyra's blood ran cold. Corvus had found them.

She had led them straight to the heart of the underworld.

With a desperate glance at Jax, she knew their only option was to fight their way out or face the consequences of possessing a forbidden symphony.

Chapter 4: A Symphony of Screams

Panic surged through Lyra as Corvus agents stormed the bar, their faces grim under harsh neon lights.

Jax, his cybernetic eye flashing red, slammed his fist on the table, sending a spray of ale flying.

He grabbed a chipped mug, brandishing it like a makeshift weapon.

"Looks like we're playing a different tune tonight," he growled, a note of grim humor in his voice.

Lyra's mind raced.

Escape was the only option, but the bar's single exit was blocked by two imposing figures in black armor.

She darted under a table, adrenaline coursing through her veins. The cacophony of shouts and shattering glass drowned out her fear as a brawl erupted.

Through the chaos, she watched as Jax, surprisingly agile for his size, fought back with ferocious intensity.

He disarmed one agent, using his cybernetic eye to emit a blinding flash of light, the other agent screaming in pain.

However, two more agents rushed him, pinning him to the floor with brutal efficiency.

Lyra knew then they were cornered.

Despair threatened to engulf her, but a flicker of defiance sparked within her.

This fight wasn't just about the music; it was about standing up to oppression.

Taking a deep breath, she remembered her violin case.

It wasn't just a container, it was an instrument.

Her fingers brushed against the hidden compartment, feeling the outline of the fragment.

There was power in the music, even a single piece.

Taking a chance, she unlatched the case.

Just as an agent lunged for her, she held up the violin.

"Don't touch me!" she cried, her voice surprisingly steady.

"This music... it's more dangerous than you know."

A look of confusion flitted across the agent's face.

She had gambled on his ignorance of the fragment's true nature.

Taking a deep breath, she closed her eyes and began to play.

It wasn't a complete melody, just the fragment passed down by her grandmother.

But as the first notes filled the air, a hush fell over the room.

A stunned silence descended upon the brawl, both agents and patrons alike captivated by the raw emotion pouring from the music.

The fragment, a single piece of a revolution, conveyed an overwhelming sense of defiance and longing.

It spoke of a world yearning for freedom, a world where art could flourish without constraints.

As the final note faded, the room remained suspended in an eerie silence.

Lyra, her heart pounding, opened her eyes.

The Corvus agents stood frozen, their faces pale and expressionless.

Then, with a jolt, the cybernetic eye of the agent restraining Jax flickered erratically.

With a strangled cry, the agent stumbled back, clutching his head.

The other agent mirrored the reaction, both of them collapsing to the floor in a heap.

Jax, bewildered but free, stared at Lyra, then at the violin. "What did you do?" he rasped.

Lyra didn't have time to explain.

A wave of nausea washed over her, the power of the music taking its toll.

She sank to her knees, clutching the violin case, the fragment within burning against her skin.

Before she could succumb to the overwhelming emotion, a hand grabbed her arm.

It was Jax, his face etched with a mixture of worry and something akin to awe.

"Come on," he grunted, pulling her toward the back of the bar.

A hidden door creaked open, revealing a narrow, dust-filled tunnel.

"This way," he whispered, urgency lacing his voice. "We need to get out of here."

Lyra stumbled through the tunnel, adrenaline keeping her legs moving.

Behind them, the bar echoed with the sounds of bewildered patrons stirring back to life.

The symphony, even a fragment, had proven its power, not just to inspire but to disrupt, to sow doubt in the hearts of Corvus' enforcers.

They had escaped by a hair's breadth, but the journey had just begun.

The symphony's secrets lay within reach, and with them, the potential to ignite a rebellion far greater than anyone could have imagined.

Chapter 5: Echoes in the Dark

LYRA STUMBLED OUT OF the dusty tunnel, blinking in the harsh sunlight.

The grimy alley behind the bar reeked of stale garbage and forgotten dreams.

Jax, his movements surprisingly agile for his size, followed close behind, his cybernetic eye flickering erratically.

"That was..." he began, his voice hoarse, then stopped, searching for the right words.

Lyra, still shaken by the symphony's unexpected power, leaned against the grimy brick wall.

The violin case felt heavy in her hand, a physical manifestation of the burden and the potential she now carried.

"It worked," she whispered, more to herself than Jax.

The fragment, a single note of defiance, had disrupted the Corvus agents, momentarily breaking their ironclad control.

But how much control did she truly have over such a powerful melody?

And what were the consequences of wielding it?

Jax, ever practical, pulled her out of her reverie.

"We need to move," he said, his voice low and urgent.

"Corvus won't take kindly to their agents being incapacitated by a fiddle and a pretty face."

Lyra winced at his bluntness, but she knew he was right.

News of the incident would spread like wildfire through the underbelly of the city.

Corvus would be relentless in their pursuit, determined to silence the music and anyone associated with it.

"Where do we go?" she asked, a knot of apprehension tightening in her stomach.

Jax looked around, his eyes scanning the maze of buildings like a seasoned scavenger.

"There's an abandoned comm relay station on the outskirts," he said, pointing towards a cluster of decaying skyscrapers.

"It's a neutral zone, even Corvus doesn't bother with it."

A neutral zone.

The term sounded more like an oxymoron in a world controlled by Corvus.

But it was their only option for now.

They navigated the labyrinthine streets, the oppressive weight of Corvus' omnipresent surveillance hovering over them.

Every flickering security camera and every holographic advertisement felt like a judging eye, searching for them.

Lyra clutched the violin case tighter, her fingers tracing the outline of the fragment within.

The melody it held echoed in her mind, a constant reminder of the fight ahead.

This wasn't just about her music anymore; it was about a rebellion waiting to be ignited, a fight for artistic freedom that had been brewing for decades.

As they reached the outskirts of the city, the towering skyscrapers gave way to a desolate landscape of rusting factories and abandoned construction sites.

The comm relay station loomed in the distance, a skeletal structure with its antennae pointing accusingly toward the smog-choked sky.

Just as they approached the station, a glint of light caught Lyra's eye.

A lone figure stood atop a pile of rubble, silhouetted against the setting sun.

Jax stopped abruptly, his hand instinctively reaching for the hidden weapon strapped to his thigh.

"Who's there?"

Jax called out, his voice a low growl.

The figure remained silent, unmoving. A sense of foreboding washed over Lyra.

This wasn't a good sign.

Had Corvus already tracked them down?

Or was this something else entirely, something far more dangerous?

As the figure slowly descended from the rubble pile, moonlight finally illuminated their face.

Lyra's breath hitched in her throat.

It was a woman, her features obscured by a tattered hood, but the fiery crimson hair cascading down her back was unmistakable.

It was Anya Sharma, the scholar who had revealed the secrets of the symphony.

But Dr. Sharma's eyes, usually filled with a lifetime of knowledge, now held a chilling emptiness.

Her voice, devoid of its usual warmth, echoed through the desolate landscape.

"Welcome, Lyra Vance," Dr. Sharma said, a hint of a smile playing on her lips.

"We've been expecting you."

Lyra's heart plummeted into her stomach.

This wasn't a reunion, it was a trap.

The scholar who had guided her, who had ignited the spark of rebellion, now stood against her, her eyes reflecting a sinister purpose.

And as Dr. Sharma spoke further, her words confirmed Lyra's worst fears.

"Corvus doesn't just control art," she said, her voice dripping with chilling enthusiasm.

"It controls people too."

Chapter 6: Discordant Harmony

LYRA'S MIND REELED.

Dr. Sharma, the one person she trusted, the beacon of knowledge and hope in her quest, was a pawn of Corvus?

Her heart hammered against her ribs, a frantic drum solo against the chilling silence of the abandoned comm relay station.

Jax, ever-reactionary, lunged toward the corrupted scholar.

With a snarl, he unleashed a flurry of punches, but Dr. Sharma, her movements surprisingly agile, effortlessly deflected them.

A glint of metal flashed as she whipped out a vibroblade, its serrated edge buzzing with a menacing hum.

"Don't be a fool," Dr. Sharma said, her voice devoid of emotion. "Corvus can offer you so much more than a life of rebellion."

Jax ignored her, fueled by anger and betrayal.

But the fight was uneven.

Dr. Sharma, augmented by unknown technology, moved like a phantom, each attack precise and lethal.

Jax stumbled back, clutching his arm, a crimson stain blooming on his sleeve.

Lyra couldn't stand by and watch.

Grasping the violin case, she threw it at Dr. Sharma, hoping to create a distraction.

The case thudded against the woman's shoulder, momentarily breaking her focus.

Jax seized the opportunity, lunging once more, his desperate attack forcing Dr. Sharma to retreat.

They huddled together, adrenaline and fear coursing through them.

"She... she's not Dr. Sharma," Lyra stammered, her voice tight with terror.

Jax grimaced, his face pale.

"Corvus tech," he spat, wiping blood from his wound.

"They can reprogram people, twist them into loyal puppets."

The revelation sent a shiver down Lyra's spine.

The thought of Dr. Sharma, the wise scholar, twisted into a mindless Corvus soldier was horrifying.

But it also explained her cryptic words about Corvus's control.

"We need to get out of here," Jax rasped, his voice strained.

"They'll have reinforcements on the way."

They darted through the maze of ruined structures, Dr. Sharma's chilling laughter echoing behind them.

The desolate landscape offered little cover, and her augmented abilities granted her an unnatural speed.

Lyra, desperate for a plan, remembered the fragment in its hidden compartment.

Could the music somehow counter Dr. Sharma's enhanced state?

It was a gamble, but they had no other choice.

Reaching a derelict building, they took cover behind crumbling walls.

Jax, despite his injury, kept watch while Lyra fumbled with the violin case.

With a frantic breath, she unlatched it, pulling out the fragment.

Taking a deep breath, she closed her eyes and began to play.

The melody, raw and incomplete, echoed within the decaying structure.

It was a desperate plea, a call to arms against the suffocating grip of Corvus.

As the music filled the air, a strange thing happened.

Dr. Sharma, who had been relentless in her pursuit, halted mid-stride.

Her movements became erratic, her face contorted in pain.

The vibroblade clattered to the ground with a metallic clang.

Jax stared, bewildered. "What's happening?"

Lyra continued to play, pouring her emotions, her fear, and her hope into the fragment.

The music swelled, a discordant harmony battling against the Corvus technology that held Dr. Sharma captive.

With a final, agonizing scream, Dr. Sharma collapsed to the ground.

The corrupted look in her eyes vanished, replaced by confusion and a flicker of recognition.

Lyra stopped playing, the fragment trembling in her hand. Dr. Sharma, weak and disoriented, looked up at her.

"Lyra?" she croaked, her voice raspy. "What... what happened?"

Tears welled up in Lyra's eyes. Relief and trepidation battled within her.

"We need to get you out of here," she said, her voice thick with emotion.

As they helped Dr. Sharma to her feet, a squad of Corvus enforcers materialized around them, their faces grim under glowing visors.

"There you are," one of them boomed, his voice amplified by his helmet.

"You'll come with us quietly."

Lyra glanced at Jax, their eyes filled with defiance.

The fragment, a beacon of hope, felt heavy in her hand.

Corvus might have repurposed Dr. Sharma, but they hadn't silenced the symphony.

The melody, even a fragment, held the power to disrupt, to break control, and perhaps, to spark a rebellion that would shake the very foundations of the oppressive regime.

Chapter 7: Echoes in the Storm

"NOT A CHANCE," JAX growled, his hand already on the hilt of his hidden vibroblade.

The Corvus enforcers, clad in their menacing black armor, tightened their formation, their visors reflecting the harsh moonlight-like emotionless eyes.

Lyra clutched the violin case tighter, the worn leather a grounding force against the rising tide of fear.

Dr. Sharma, still dazed from Corvus's mind control, stood behind them, a fragile figure caught in the crossfire.

Escape seemed impossible, yet surrender was unthinkable.

A tense silence stretched between them, broken only by the rasping breaths of the wounded Jax and the rhythmic hum of the distant city.

Then, with a cold glint in his visor, the lead enforcer spoke.

"Stand down and relinquish the fragment," he commanded, his voice a metallic monotone.

"Resistance is futile."

Lyra glanced at Jax, their eyes meeting in a silent exchange.

They wouldn't give up without a fight.

This wasn't just about the music; it was a stand against the stifling control that had choked the galaxy for decades.

"We won't be silenced," Lyra declared, her voice surprisingly steady.

"The symphony will be heard!"

As if in response to her words, a low rumble echoed in the distance.

The ground began to tremble, sending dust swirling from the decaying buildings.

The Corvus enforcers exchanged confused glances.

Then, from the edge of the city, a sight both majestic and terrifying emerged.

It was a massive scavenger freighter, its hull adorned with a sprawling mural depicting a shattered violin spewing forth vibrant music notes.

On its bridge, a figure stood silhouetted against the smog-choked sky, a speaker held aloft.

"Attention Corvus scum!" boomed a powerful voice, crackling across the wasteland.

"This is Captain Reyes of the 'Discordant Harmony,' and you've just stumbled into a rebellion!"

Relief washed over Lyra.

The Scavengers Guild was alerted by Dr. Sharma's encrypted message before her capture had arrived.

But the surprise wasn't one-sided.

The Corvus enforcers caught off guard, scrambled to secure their weapons.

Lyra saw her opportunity.

With a swift movement, she slipped the fragment from the violin case and tucked it into Jax's hand.

"Get it to the freighter," she whispered, urgency lacing her voice.

"Find Reyes, she knows what to do."

Jax, understanding the weight of the request, nodded resolutely.

Before the enforcers could react, he darted across the ruins, his injured arm throbbing with every step.

The Corvus enforcers opened fire, the wasteland erupting in a symphony of laser beams and the metallic clang of Jax's vibroblade deflecting them.

Lyra, fueled by a surge of adrenaline, grabbed her violin. It wasn't a weapon, but it was the only thing she had.

She charged, not at the enforcers, but at the comm relay station's central control tower.

With a flying leap, she scaled the crumbling structure, adrenaline fueling her every move.

Reaching the control panel, she slammed her fist onto the activation button.

The station, long dormant, sputtered to life.

A wave of static crackled through the comms network, momentarily disrupting Corvus's carefully controlled broadcasts.

Then, through the distorted static, Lyra began to play.

The fragment, raw and powerful, resonated through the airwaves, a defiant challenge to Corvus's bland, monotonous music.

As she played, the Discordant Harmony unleashed a volley of sonic disrupters, beams of concentrated sound that momentarily disoriented the Corvus agents.

The battle raged below.

Jax, a whirlwind of determination, fought his way toward the freighter, the Corvus enforcers hot on his heels.

The Discordant Harmony's crew, a motley collection of scavengers and rebels, rained down fire from the ship's cannons.

Lyra, perched atop the control tower, poured her heart into the music.

The fragment, meant to be a single note in a grand symphony, became a beacon of hope, a cry for freedom that resonated across the wasteland and beyond.

With a final, desperate flourish, the fragment ended.

Exhausted but exhilarated, Lyra collapsed onto the control panel.

Below, the battle reached a crescendo.

Jax, battered but alive, clambered aboard the Discordant Harmony as the freighter began to lift off.

The Corvus enforcers, their comms disrupted and their formation broken, were forced to retreat.

The symphony, even a fragment, had disrupted their control, a testament to its raw power.

As the Discordant Harmony roared into the night sky, Lyra watched, a single tear tracing a path down her cheek.

The fight was far from over, but a spark had been ignited.

Chapter 8: Discordant Harmony Takes Flight

———

THE DISCORDANT HARMONY, a hodgepodge of scavenged parts and unyielding spirit hummed with newfound purpose.

Lyra and Jax welcomed aboard with a mixture of curiosity and skepticism, found themselves amidst a motley crew.

Captain Reyes, a woman with fiery red hair and a cybernetic eye that mirrored Jax's, surveyed them with a piercing gaze.

"So," she drawled, her voice like gravel grinding against metal, "you two managed to cause quite a stir using a fiddle and a memory."

Lyra, still reeling from the encounter with the Corvus enforcers, nodded hesitantly. "The fragment... it had an effect. They retreated, even if..."

Jax, ever the pragmatist, cut her off. "Even if it's temporary. Corvus doesn't give up easily."

Captain Reyes chuckled a harsh sound that echoed through the ship's cramped control room.

"No, they certainly don't. But they don't expect a rusty freighter full of misfits and a dreamer with a broken violin to be their biggest headache."

Her gaze returned to Lyra, a hint of respect flickering within.

"So, dreamer, what's the plan with that fragment?

You got a whole symphony locked inside that thing?"

Lyra shook her head.

"No, only a single note. But Dr. Sharma... she mentioned other fragments scattered across the galaxy."

Captain Reyes raised an eyebrow.

"Sounds like a scavenger hunt on a galactic scale. Dangerous, but then again, what isn't these days?"

A tense silence settled over the room.

The weight of their mission, the potential for failure, hung heavy in the air.

But Jax broke the silence, a spark of defiance lighting his eyes.

"We may be misfits, but we've got nothing to lose," he said, his voice rough with determination. "And a galaxy full of silent voices yearning to be heard."

A murmur of agreement rippled through the crew.

These weren't just smugglers and rogues; they were survivors, artists who had hidden their talents to escape Corvus' oppression.

Lyra saw a glimmer of hope in their eyes, a spark rekindled by the defiance carried on the fragment's melody.

Captain Reyes slammed her fist on the control panel.

"Alright," she declared, her voice ringing with newfound resolve.

"We find those fragments, kid. We turn that single note into a full-blown symphony. One loud enough to deafen Corvus and awaken the galaxy."

The decision was made.

The Discordant Harmony, once a scavenger vessel, became a vessel of rebellion.

Lyra thrust into the role of unlikely leader, studied Dr. Sharma's cryptic notes, searching for clues to the location of the other fragments.

Jax, his cybernetic eye scanning intercepted Corvus's transmissions and became their lookout, ever vigilant for signs of pursuit.

Meanwhile, the crew, their talents rekindled, began weaving fantastical tales and composing rebellious songs, their creativity blooming in the freighter's cramped quarters.

The journey was fraught with danger.

They navigated asteroid fields teeming with Corvus patrols, bartered with shady informants in hidden spaceports, and even escaped a near-death encounter with a monstrous space Kraken (a tale Captain Reyes embellished with every retelling).

As they ventured deeper into the galaxy, they encountered pockets of resistance, whispers of rebellion echoing in the darkness.

A hidden colony of artists who broadcast coded messages through their paintings.

A musician who defied Corvus with a silent symphony played on bioluminescent insects.

These encounters fueled their determination, reminding them that their fight was bigger than a single broken violin.

Finally, after weeks of perilous travel, Dr. Sharma's notes led them to a desolate moon orbiting a gas giant.

The coordinates pointed to a crumbling research facility, a relic of a forgotten age.

It was here, amidst the ruins of past innovation, that they hoped to find the second fragment.

Lyra, her heart pounding with anticipation, led the way.

The facility, shrouded in an eerie silence, was a maze of dusty corridors and malfunctioning machinery.

As they ventured deeper, the air grew heavier, choked with the dust of forgotten dreams.

Then, amidst a display of ancient instruments, they found it.

A small, crystalline disc, shimmering with an otherworldly light.

As Lyra reached out to touch it, a wave of energy pulsed through the room, activating dormant machinery. Holographic screens flickered to life, revealing a face from the past, a composer whose name had been erased by Corvus.

"The symphony," the voice echoed, ethereal and powerful, "is a weapon of freedom.

Let its music break the chains of conformity and ignite the flame of rebellion within every soul."

The holographic figure faded, leaving Lyra and her companions bathed in the ethereal glow of the fragment.

A profound silence filled the chamber, broken only by the ragged breaths of the crew.

Jax, ever the pragmatist, was the first to speak.

"So, a weapon, huh? Now that's a symphony I can get behind."

Captain Reyes, a glint of steely determination in her eyes, nodded.

"We've got the first two notes. Time to turn this rebellion up a notch."

Lyra, overwhelmed by the weight of the message and the responsibility it placed upon her, held the fragment close.

The music within pulsed with raw power, a symphony waiting to be unleashed.

It wasn't just about defiance anymore; it was about igniting a revolution, a fight for the very soul of art itself.

"Let's go home," she declared, her voice ringing with newfound resolve.

"Let's turn the galaxy into a concert hall, and let the symphony be heard."

The crew of the Discordant Harmony erupted in cheers.

They weren't just misfits and dreamers anymore; they were warriors armed with a melody, the vanguard of a rebellion that would shake the foundations of Corvus' oppressive regime.

As they hurried back to the freighter, the desolate moon echoed with the faint strains of music, a whisper of the symphony yet to come.

It was a challenge, a promise, and a spark of hope that would resonate across the galaxy, inspiring the silent voices to rise and sing their own defiant songs.

The fight for artistic freedom had entered a new phase, and the Discordant Harmony, with its unlikely conductor and its powerful weapon of music, was ready to lead the charge.

The galaxy would never be the same.

Chapter 9: Echoes of Betrayal

The Discordant Harmony, a ramshackle freighter now christened the "Symphony of Defiance," hurtled through the black void, its engines straining against the pull of an uncharted nebula.

Inside, a tense silence clung to the air, thick enough to choke on.

Lyra, her fingers drumming a nervous rhythm on the violin case, studied the cryptic message flickering on the control panel.

"Warning: High-density anomaly detected. Deviation from programmed course advised."

The red warning text pulsed a sinister rhythm, mirroring the frantic beat of Lyra's heart.

Dr. Sharma's decrypted coordinates, believed to hold the third fragment, led them here, into this swirling mass of cosmic dust and plasma storms.

Jax, his cybernetic eye scanning the swirling nebula on the holographic map, muttered a curse.

"We're blind in here, Lyra. Sensors are useless. Flying into this... it's suicide."

Captain Reyes, a grim line etched across her battle-hardened face, slammed her fist on the control panel.

"We can't turn back," she growled. "Every lost day is another day Corvus tightens its grip. We need that fragment."

Lyra understood.

Each fragment added another note to their symphony, another weapon in their fight against artistic oppression.

But a nagging doubt gnawed at her.

Dr. Sharma's notes, recovered after the Corvus attack, seemed... off. Vague, almost hastily scribbled.

A shiver ran down her spine.

Could Dr. Sharma, still recovering from Corvus' mind control, have made a mistake?

Or was this a trap, a cleverly disguised lure leading them to their doom?

Suddenly, a sickening jolt rocked the ship.

Alarms blared, red lights strobing in a frantic panic.

Jax swore, his grip tightening on the control handles.

"We've hit something! Shields are failing!"

The ship lurched violently, throwing everyone off balance.

Lyra scrambled to her feet, adrenaline surging through her veins.

Through the viewport, a horrifying sight unfolded.

They hadn't hit an asteroid; it was a colossal Corvus battleship, its sleek armor glinting menacingly in the nebula's swirling light.

"They were waiting for us," Captain Reyes snarled, her voice grim.

"The message... it was a trap."

Lyra felt a wave of nausea.

Betrayal.

Dr. Sharma, the one person they trusted, the one who had guided them, had led them straight into an ambush.

Was it a relapse of Corvus' control, or something more sinister?

The questions swirled in her mind, lost in the chaos that erupted around her.

Corvus fighters swarmed around the Symphony of Defiance, peppering the freighter with laser fire.

Sparks erupted as the shields sputtered, their energy reserves rapidly depleting.

Jax fought valiantly at the helm, dodging fire, desperately searching for an escape route.

But the nebula, once their refuge, was now their prison.

Their haphazard navigation had left them trapped within the dense plasma storms, their cloak rendered useless.

It was a calculated move by Corvus, a display of ruthless efficiency that sent a cold dread down Lyra's spine.

As the ship shuddered under another barrage, Captain Reyes made a harsh decision.

"Abandon ship! Everyone to the escape pods!"

Lyra's heart plummeted.

The escape pods were old and barely maintained, and the nebula was a swirling death trap.

The odds of survival were slim.

The crew scrambled toward the escape pods, fear etched on their faces.

Lyra, however, hesitated.

She clutched the violin case, the fragment within its worn leather radiating an unexpected warmth.

They couldn't let Corvus win.

This wasn't just about survival; it was about the fight, about the symphony.

Just then, Jax grabbed her arm, his face grim.

"Lyra, there's no time! Trust me, this isn't over!"

He shoved her towards the nearest escape pod, a fierce determination burning in his eyes.

With a final, desperate glance at the burning freighter, Lyra entered the pod.

The hatch slammed shut, and she found herself hurtling towards the swirling nebula, a single tear tracing a path down her cheek.

The Symphony of Defiance, their home, their symbol of rebellion, was engulfed in flames, taking with it not only their hopes but a vital fragment of the symphony.

Lyra felt a scream rise in her throat, but it died on her lips.

She couldn't let despair consume her.

Jax, the crew, even Dr. Sharma's true intentions – everything was shrouded in uncertainty. But one thing remained clear.

The symphony wasn't just music; it was a weapon, a language understood by a consciousness far vaster than anything she'd ever imagined.

The information overload threatened to overwhelm her, but a single thought pierced through the chaos.

The betrayal.

Dr. Sharma.

The hooded figure seemed to sense her confusion.

"The doctor," it spoke, its voice a calming hum, "was a pawn, a conduit. Corvus' control only scratched the surface. She is... recovering."

Lyra's head spun.

Dr. Sharma, manipulated but not entirely lost?

The revelation sparked a flicker of hope amidst the whirlwind of questions.

Suddenly, a new image flooded her mind, a vision of a colossal structure pulsating with an otherworldly light – the heart of Corvus' control.

And within it, a single, corrupted note, a distortion of the symphony's true harmony.

It was the source of their oppression.

Lyra gasped, the weight of the revelation settling on her shoulders.

This wasn't just about finding the remaining fragments and completing the symphony.

They needed to reach the heart of Corvus and rectify the corrupted note, to silence the discord and unleash the symphony's true power.

Tears welled up in her eyes, a mixture of fear and newfound resolve.

The symphony, once a beacon of hope, now carried a weight far greater than she could have ever imagined.

It was the key not only to artistic freedom but to the liberation of a galaxy held captive by a corrupted melody.

Taking a shaky breath, Lyra released the violin case.

It wasn't just a protective shell anymore; it felt like a conductor's baton, a symbol of the responsibility that now rested in her hands.

"I... I understand," she whispered, her voice hoarse but firm.

"The symphony... it needs to be played."

The hooded figure smiled, a luminescent glow emanating from beneath the hood. "Then let us begin, child.

The galaxy waits for its true song to be heard."

As the cavern pulsed with a renewed light, and the figures around her began to chant in an unknown yet strangely familiar language, Lyra knew this was just the beginning.

The fight for artistic freedom had taken a dramatic turn, and she, a simple violinist thrust into the role of conductor, was now at the heart of a rebellion that could reshape the very essence of the galaxy.

Chapter 10: Whispers in the Dark

LYRA PLUMMETED THROUGH the churning nebula, the escape pod buffeted by violent gusts of plasma wind.

Tears blurred her vision, a kaleidoscope of emotions – grief for the lost Symphony of Defiance, rage at the betrayal, and a gnawing fear for Jax and the crew.

But amidst the chaos, a spark of defiance flickered within her.

They couldn't lose.

Not yet.

The escape pod lurched violently, alarms blaring.

A critical systems failure warning flashed crimson on the control panel.

Lyra, with no piloting experience, gripped the controls, her heart hammering against her ribs.

She had to get out of the nebula, and find any semblance of safety.

Suddenly, a booming voice crackled over the comms.

Static-laden, but unmistakable – Captain Reyes.

"Lyra! Can you hear me? You're off course! Steer toward the coordinates I'm sending now! It's a hidden outpost... our last hope!"

Hope, however, was a fragile thing in this unforgiving environment. Lyra wrestled with the controls, the pod groaning in protest as she fought to follow the erratic trajectory on the holographic map.

As they plunged deeper into the nebula, the darkness seemed to press in, the silence broken only by the groaning of the pod and the frantic thump of her own heart. Then, amidst the swirling chaos, a flicker appeared on the long-range scanner. A faint blip, barely registering, but a potential lifeline.

With a burst of renewed energy, Lyra adjusted course. As they neared the blip, the scanner image sharpened, revealing a massive, asteroid-sized object, its surface riddled with cavernous openings. It wasn't a space station; it was a colossal, dormant space whale, its bioluminescent markings pulsing faintly.

A sudden jolt rocked the pod. The warning lights intensified, followed by a deafening silence. Dead silence. Lyra's breath caught in her throat. Engine failure. They were hurtling towards the space whale with no means of control.

Bracing for impact, she closed her eyes, the fragment in its worn case clutched tightly in her hand. This was it. The end.

But the end didn't come. Instead, a gentle rumble resonated through the pod, followed by an unnerving sensation of being caught in a web. Lyra opened her eyes to see the pod suspended mid-air, entangled in a mass of shimmering, bioluminescent threads emanating from the space whale's surface.

Panic threatened to consume her, but then, a voice echoed within her mind, soft, melodic, yet strangely familiar. "Welcome, child of the symphony. We have been waiting."

Lyra's eyes widened. Was she hallucinating? The voice spoke again, its tone gentle yet insistent. "Do not fear. The symphony lives. And it has a new movement to play."

The escape pod gently lowered onto the surface of the space whale, the bioluminescent threads retracting silently. With trembling hands, Lyra unbuckled her harness and stepped out onto a platform of smooth, cold rock.

Before her, the vast cavern within the space whale's body pulsed with an otherworldly light. Silhouettes moved within the shadows, figures both humanoid and strangely alien. And then, a figure emerged, cloaked in luminescent robes, its face obscured by a hood.

"Dr. Sharma?" Lyra's voice echoed in the cavern, a whisper of disbelief laced with fear.

The figure tilted its head, the hood shifting to reveal a face that sent a shiver down Lyra's spine. It wasn't Dr. Sharma. But the eyes... the eyes held a familiar flicker of recognition.

"We are not Dr. Sharma," the figure spoke, its voice a melodious chime that resonated within Lyra's mind. "We are the Keepers of the Symphony. And you, child, hold a key."

The figure extended a hand, its palm glowing with an ethereal light. Lyra hesitated, her mind a whirlwind of questions and doubts. Was this another trap? Was this the true purpose of Dr. Sharma's cryptic notes?

Taking a deep breath, fueled by desperate hope and the weight of the unfinished symphony, Lyra extended her own hand, clutching the violin case in a white-knuckled grip.

But as their hands met, a jolt of energy surged through her, an avalanche of information flooding her mind... and a horrifying realization.

The vision wasn't of Corvus' central control. It was of the escape pod, moments before its descent into the nebula. The hooded figure, was not a benevolent keeper, but a chilling spectre of Dr. Sharma, her eyes glowing with a malevolent green light that mirrored Jax's cybernetic eye.

The realization slammed into Lyra with the force of a collapsing star.

Dr. Sharma, not a victim of Corvus control, but a willing participant.

Worse, an architect of the betrayal.

The cryptic notes, the coordinates leading to the nebula – all an elaborate trap orchestrated by Corvus, using a familiar face to manipulate them.

Chapter 11: A Discordant Note

Lyra gasped, the shock ripping through her like a sonic blast.

The vision wasn't of Corvus' control center, but of the escape pod itself.

And the hooded figure – not a benevolent keeper, but a chilling spectre of Dr. Sharma, her eyes glowing with a malevolent green light that mirrored Jax's cybernetic eye.

The revelation slammed into Lyra with the force of a collapsing star.

Dr. Sharma, not a victim of Corvus control, but a willing participant.

Worse, an architect of the betrayal.

The cryptic notes, the coordinates leading to the nebula – all an elaborate trap orchestrated by Corvus, using a familiar face to manipulate them.

The cavern floor lurched beneath her feet, the bioluminescent glow pulsating with a sinister rhythm.

The whispers of the figures around her, once melodic, now sounded like a twisted chorus, mocking her naivety.

Dr. Sharma's voice, laced with a chilling amusement, echoed within her mind.

"Surprised, Lyra? The symphony thrives on discord, and your trust was the sweetest note of all."

Lyra stumbled back, her heart pounding a frantic tattoo against her ribs.

The fragment in her case, once a beacon of hope, now felt heavy, a cursed object manipulated by a deranged mind.

"You see," Dr. Sharma continued, her voice dripping with malicious glee, "the symphony needs a conductor.

And you, with your misplaced trust and broken violin, were perfect."

Rage, a primal roar, surged through Lyra.

They had played her like a cheap instrument, their goal not just to destroy the Symphony of Defiance, but to twist her into a pawn for their own twisted agenda.

But amidst the fury, a flicker of defiance sparked.

They might have broken her violin, but they couldn't break her spirit.

The symphony, even incomplete, held a power they underestimated.

"You want a conductor?" she roared, her voice echoing through the cavern.

"Then you'll get one!"

Lyra flung open the violin case, its worn leather protesting.

The fragment within didn't radiate warmth anymore; it pulsed with a cold, angry light. But it was power nonetheless.

With trembling hands, she pulled out the fragment, not to play a melody, but to channel its raw energy.

Focusing all her anger, on her defiance, she slammed the fragment against the cavern wall.

The bioluminescent glow flickered, the cavern trembling under an unseen force.

A scream, digitized and laced with pain, ripped through the cave, emanating from the hooded figure.

Dr. Sharma's illusion flickered, revealing a cybernetic core embedded beneath the robes, pulsing with a malevolent light.

Corvus.

It wasn't Dr. Sharma at all, but a sophisticated Corvus agent, using her memories and appearance as a weapon.

And the bioluminescent threads that had entangled the escape pod – not a haven, but a control mechanism.

The cavern echoed with chaos as the other figures, revealed to be Corvus androids, scrambled to contain the surge of energy.

Lyra, seizing the opportunity, turned and ran, the fragment clutched tightly in her hand.

The escape pod, a symbol of their betrayal, hung limply from the bioluminescent threads.

But escape wasn't an option.

Not anymore.

Not with the truth laid bare.

She had to warn Jax, the crew, and anyone who might still be alive.

They had to regroup, to understand the true enemy and its power.

The symphony, incomplete as it was, had become a weapon, a beacon for the rebellion. But it could also be a trap, a tool to manipulate and control.

Lyra weaved through the cavern, dodging tendrils of bioluminescent energy that lashed out like angry serpents.

Her mind raced, formulating a plan, a desperate gambit against a seemingly invincible force.

They needed to find the remaining fragments, not to complete the symphony, but to understand its true power.

To dissect it, to rewrite its discordant notes, and use them against Corvus.

The fight had just begun, and the battlefield was no longer just the vast expanse of the galaxy, but the very essence of music itself.

As she burst out of the cavern, the nebula swirling above, Lyra knew one thing for certain.

The symphony wouldn't be silenced.

It would be rewritten, transformed into a weapon of defiance, a discordant anthem that would shatter Corvus' control and awaken the galaxy to a new rhythm – the rhythm of rebellion.

Chapter 12: Echoes in the Wreckage

LYRA STUMBLED OUT OF the space whale's cavern, the chilling realization of Dr. Sharma's betrayal clinging to her like a shroud.

The nebula swirled above, a chaotic tapestry of churning gas and plasma storms.

The escape pod, their mangled symbol of hope, dangled limply from bioluminescent threads – a stark reminder of Corvus' manipulative grip.

Tears welled up in her eyes, blurring the already treacherous landscape.

Grief for Jax, the crew, and the shattered remains of the Symphony of Defiance threatened to consume her.

But amidst the despair, a spark of defiance flickered.

They wouldn't win through blind faith anymore.

They needed a new plan, a deeper understanding of the symphony and its true power.

She gripped the fragment in its worn case, its cold surface a stark contrast to the warmth it had once radiated.

This wasn't just a musical note; it was a weapon, a key that could unlock the symphony's secrets.

But how?

Where to begin?

Suddenly, a flicker on her long-range scanner caught her eye.

A faint distress signal, barely registering amidst the nebula's static.

Hope flared, a fragile flame in the darkness.

Could it be Jax, or perhaps another survivor from the Symphony of Defiance?

Fuelled by a renewed sense of purpose, Lyra adjusted the escape pod's controls, ignoring the warnings flashing on the console.

This wasn't a high-tech vessel, but it was her only chance.

She hurtled towards the faint signal, the nebula's turbulence rocking the pod like a toy in a bathtub.

As she neared the source, the distress signal grew stronger, resolving into a garbled transmission. "...anyone out there... This is Captain Reyes... Ship in distress... Lost in the storm..."

Captain Reyes!

Relief flooded through Lyra, washing away some of the oppressive despair.

The captain was alive, and if she was out there, so could be others.

The signal led her to a wreckage field, a graveyard of spaceships caught in the nebula's violent dance.

Debris shimmered amidst the swirling gas clouds, twisted metal monuments to Corvus' ruthless efficiency.

Lyra cautiously navigated the wreckage, her heart pounding in her chest.

Spotting a glimmer of light amidst the debris, she steered the escape pod closer.

It was the mangled remains of a Corvus fighter, sparks leaping erratically from its exposed wiring.

And next to it, battered but alive, stood Captain Reyes, her face streaked with grease and grime, but her cybernetic eye burning with a familiar defiance.

"Lyra!"

Captain Reyes barked, her voice hoarse with exhaustion.

"You're alive! Thank the stars! I thought... I thought we lost you."

Lyra didn't waste time with pleasantries.

"Captain, we need to get out of here. Dr. Sharma... she was... working with Corvus. It was all a trap."

Reyes' face hardened.

"Sharma? That... that manipulative snake! I knew something was off."

Relief washed over Lyra, a sense of validation for her suspicions.

She recounted her encounter with the space whale, the chilling revelation of Dr.

Sharma's true allegiance.

"So, Corvus wants the symphony too, huh?"

Captain Reyes muttered, stroking her scarred chin.

"Figures. But they won't get their hands on it. Not while I still draw breath."

Lyra nodded, a fierce determination mirroring itself in the captain's gaze.

They were battered, their resources dwindling, but their spirit remained unbroken.

The symphony, once a beacon of hope for artistic freedom, had become a weapon in a far more complex war.

"We need a plan, Captain," Lyra declared, her voice ringing with newfound resolve.

"We need to understand the symphony, its true power, and how to use it against Corvus."

Captain Reyes grinned, a flash of her old bravado returning.

"Then let's crack this thing open, kid.

We got a symphony to rewrite."

As they surveyed the wreckage field, a flicker of movement caught Lyra's eye.

Half-buried beneath twisted metal, a small, battered figure stirred.

Jax.

His face was pale, his cybernetic eye flickering erratically, but undeniably alive.

The sight brought a choked sob to Lyra's lips.

They weren't alone.

They were survivors, battered but unbowed.

And amidst the wreckage of their dreams, a new song was about to be born – a discordant symphony of rebellion, fueled by defiance and the echoes of a galaxy yearning to be heard.

Chapter 13: Echoes of Dissent

The reunion inside the cramped escape pod was a mix of tearful embraces, relieved laughter, and the ever-present hum of anxiety.

Jax, his cybernetic eye displaying a worrying flicker, recounted his harrowing escape from the Symphony of Defiance's destruction.

Miraculously, the escape pod he salvaged, though battered, remained functional.

"We can't stay here," Captain Reyes declared, her tone grim as she scanned the wreckage field.

"Corvus might have salvage drones combing the area. We need to rendezvous at the pre-determined fallback point – the abandoned research station on Kepler-186f."

A collective groan rippled through the pod. Kepler-186f, a desolate, icy world at the fringe of known space, was hardly an ideal hideout.

But it was their only hope.

The journey was arduous, a test of their resilience.

Food supplies dwindled, and the harsh radiation of the nebula took its toll, leaving them all weak and weary.

But the memory of Corvus' betrayal and the weight of the unfinished symphony fueled their determination.

As they neared Kepler-186f, a colossal, ice-covered sphere, Captain Reyes' voice crackled over the comms.

"Looks like we have company." Her words sent a jolt of fear through Lyra. Had Corvus tracked them?

Jax, ever the pragmatist, gripped the controls of the escape pod.

"We can outrun them. Let's head for the research station's underground complex. It's our best shot."

They descended towards the planet, dodging a patrol of Corvus fighters.

The desolate landscape of Kepler-186f stretched before them – a vast, frozen expanse of white and grey, broken only by the jagged peaks of ancient mountains.

The research station, a hulking, abandoned structure half-buried in ice, appeared like a forgotten tomb.

Jax expertly landed the pod in a crevice near the station's entrance. As they bundled out, the frigid air bit at their exposed skin.

The entrance, a thick metal door partially coated in ice, seemed impassable.

But Jax, with his cybernetic enhancements, quickly hacked the security system, and the door creaked open with a groan.

They descended into the station's inky blackness, relying on their headlamps to navigate the network of deserted corridors.

The air hung heavy with the smell of dust and decay, broken only by the rhythmic drip of water somewhere deep within the complex.

The research station, according to Captain Reyes' intel, had once housed a team of scientists studying the potential for artistic expression in artificial intelligence.

Perhaps, she reasoned, they might find something here that could help them understand the symphony's true power.

As they ventured deeper into the complex, a faint rhythmic hum filled the air, a melody both mesmerizing and unsettling.

Following the sound, they came to a vast chamber, its walls lined with holographic displays flickering with cryptic symbols and sheet music.

In the center of the chamber stood a massive, inactive machine, its intricate metallic coils and glowing panels hinting at a forgotten technology.

Lyra studied the symbols displayed on the holographic screens, a strange sense of familiarity washing over her.

These weren't just musical notes; they seemed to represent a complex language, a code for manipulating emotions and influencing minds.

Captain Reyes knelt before a control panel, her brow furrowed in concentration.

"This technology," she muttered, "it's not just about creating music.

It's about manipulating sound waves to evoke specific responses."

Jax, ever the engineer, began tinkering with the machine's controls.

"Looks like it's powered by some kind of energy crystal. If we can find a replacement..."

The hum in the chamber suddenly intensified, the holographic displays flashing with a blinding light.

Before they could react, a holographic figure materialized in the center of the room.

It was a woman, her features regal and severe, her eyes glowing with an ethereal blue light.

"Welcome," the figure boomed, its voice echoing through the chamber.

"You who seek to understand the symphony, I offer you knowledge, but at a cost."

Chapter 14: Echoes of the Past

The spectral figure loomed before them, its words hanging heavy in the air like a pronouncement of fate.

Fear crackled through the chamber, but Captain Reyes stepped forward, her gaze unwavering.

"Who are you?" she demanded.

"I am Aella," the figure replied, its voice laced with an ancient power.

"The creator of the technology you see before you. This machine, the Harbinger, has the power to weave emotions into sound, to shape music into a weapon of persuasion."

Lyra's heart hammered in her chest.

This was the heart of it all, the origin of the symphony's power.

But Aella's words, laden with a heavy weight, hinted at a dark purpose.

"Weapon?"

Jax scoffed, his cybernetic eye flashing a warning red.

"We're not here to conquer minds. We're trying to fight oppression."

Aella's spectral form rippled with what might have been a sigh.

"Naivete is a luxury war doesn't afford. The symphony was not created for liberation. It was a tool of unity, a way to forge a collective consciousness across a vast and diverse galaxy."

Captain Reyes raised an eyebrow.

"Unity? The galaxy's under Corvus' boot because of their twisted version of unity."

Aella's eyes narrowed.

"Corvus has taken a noble concept and twisted it to serve their desires. The symphony, in its complete form, holds the power to counter that. But to unlock its full potential, you must understand its origins."

With a wave of her hand, the holograms on the walls flickered and transformed, depicting a vibrant history.

Lyra watched in awe as scenes unfolded – vast alien civilizations, bathed in the light of binary stars, resonating with a collective harmony.

The Harbinger stood at the center, its music weaving a tapestry of understanding and unity between disparate species.

But the images darkened, showcasing the rise of dissent, whispers of rebellion against the enforced harmony.

Fear crept into the music, then anger, as factions splintered apart.

The beautiful symphony became a cacophony of discord, leading to a galactic war that shattered the fragile peace.

Aella's voice, heavy with sorrow, echoed in the chamber.

"The symphony was meant to bind, not control. But in the hands of the weak-willed, it became a weapon of division. I deactivated the Harbinger, fearing the havoc it could unleash. But now... it seems the galaxy needs its voice once more."

Silence descended as the holograms faded.

The weight of history pressed down on them.

The symphony wasn't just a weapon against Corvus; it was a reminder of a forgotten ideal – a melody of peace that had once held the galaxy together.

"So, the cost of knowledge?"

Captain Reyes finally spoke, her voice low.

Aella tilted her head.

"You must retrieve the missing fragments. Each note holds a piece of the symphony's history, its power, and its potential for corruption. Only with them can you understand the true melody and wield it responsibly."

Lyra glanced at the fragment clutched in her hand, a cold knot forming in her stomach.

This wasn't just about finding notes anymore; it was about confronting the dark legacy of the symphony and understanding its power to both heal and destroy.

The true enemy wasn't just Corvus; it was the potential for misuse embedded in the music itself.

Jax, ever the pragmatist, broke the silence.

"We need a plan then. Where are these fragments?"

Aella's form shimmered faintly.

"Their locations are encoded within the Harbinger. But to access them, you need a replacement power source. Deep within this complex, buried under layers of ice, lies an energy core from a long-lost starship. Retrieve it, and the Harbinger shall guide you."

With a final flicker, Aella's spectral form dissolved, leaving the survivors of the Symphony of Defiance alone in the echoing chamber.

The weight of the past and the uncertain future settled upon them.

They had a mission now, a renewed purpose.

But the road ahead was fraught with danger, forcing them to confront not only Corvus but the very essence of the symphony itself.

The fight for artistic freedom had taken a dramatic turn, and now they were not just rebels, but custodians of a weapon that could heal a galaxy... or fracture it further.

Chapter 15: Buried Echoes

———

THE PROSPECT OF VENTURING deeper into the bowels of the research station held little appeal, especially considering the desolate world above.

But the prospect of retrieving the lost fragments and unlocking the Harbinger's secrets outweighed their discomfort.

Jax, ever the engineer, took charge, using a combination of salvaged tools and his cybernetic enhancements to scan for the buried energy core.

The air grew colder as they descended further, the oppressive silence broken only by the rhythmic dripping of water and the whirring of Jax's scanner.

"Found something,"

Jax announced finally, pointing his scanner towards a section of the station wall where the ice buildup seemed unusually thick.

"Energy signature consistent with a power core, buried about ten meters down."

Lyra shivered, not just from the cold.

Extracting an object of unknown technology from layers of ice seemed an impossible task.

But Captain Reyes, ever resourceful, had a plan.

"We'll use controlled explosions," she explained, her eyes glinting with a fierce determination.

"Just enough to crack the ice and expose the core. Jax, can you rig something up with the escape pod's emergency thrusters?"

Jax grinned, a glint of excitement in his good eye.

"Challenge accepted, Captain."

While Jax tinkered with salvaged materials, Lyra studied the holographic maps displayed on a salvaged tablet. Aella's words echoed in her mind – retrieve the fragments, understand their power, wield it responsibly.

The weight of the task settled upon her. The fragments weren't just notes; they were echoes of a forgotten past, each with the potential to be a beacon of hope or a tool of destruction.

Hours bled into one another as Jax meticulously assembled his makeshift explosive device. Finally, with a satisfied nod, he declared himself ready.

Captain Reyes, ever cautious, double-checked the safety protocols before leading them toward the target zone.

The controlled explosion, when it came, echoed throughout the cavern, leaving behind a gaping hole in the ice wall.

A plume of ice dust settled, revealing a metallic object embedded within.

It looked like a misshapen egg, its surface pulsating with a faint blue light.

Cautiously, Captain Reyes used a makeshift grappling hook to extract the core.

As they brought it back up to the main chamber, the blue light pulsed brighter, bathing the room in an ethereal glow.

The moment they connected the core to the Harbinger, the machine hummed to life, its holographic displays flickering back into existence.

With a wave of her hand, Captain Reyes activated the interface.

"Show us the locations of the missing fragments," she commanded.

The holo displays whirred back to life, projecting a series of galactic charts.

Each chart highlighted a specific location – a desolate asteroid field, a forgotten temple on a gas giant, a lost colony ship drifting in deep space.

Lyra studied the charts, a sense of foreboding growing inside her.

These locations were scattered across the galaxy, guarded by who knew what dangers. Retrieving them wouldn't just be a test of their resilience; it would be a race against time, a desperate gamble before Corvus caught wind of their activities.

Captain Reyes, ever the leader, slammed her fist on the control panel.

"We have our mission. Let's get started."

Jax, his face grim, adjusted his cybernetic eye.

"We need a new ship, Captain. The escape pod won't take us very far."

Lyra glanced at the charts, the vast distances stretching before them.

This was no longer just a rebellion; it was a galactic odyssey, a journey into the heart of a symphony that could either liberate the galaxy or shatter it into pieces.

With a renewed sense of purpose and a heavy burden of responsibility, they set about preparing for their next move.

They were no longer just survivors; they were the custodians of a symphony that held the fate of the galaxy in its discordant notes.

Their journey had just begun, and the echoes of the past would guide them, for better or worse, toward a symphony of defiance.

Chapter 16: Echoes in the Asteroid Belt

THE DESOLATE EXPANSE of the asteroid belt stretched before them, a vast graveyard of celestial debris.

The stolen Corvus fighter, christened "The Discord" with a touch of dark humor, rumbled under their feet, its engines still humming with the faint echoes of their enemies.

Their first destination – a rogue asteroid rumored to hold the second fragment of the Symphony of Defiance.

Aella's cryptic map offered only a rough location, a flickering dot amidst the chaotic dance of asteroids.

Jax, piloting with his usual reckless skill, navigated the treacherous landscape.

Lyra, co-pilot and navigator, her head buried in salvaged Corvus charts, scanned for anomalies that might match Aella's description.

"Captain," her voice crackled over the comms, "there! Up ahead. Unusual magnetic signature. Could be it."

Jax executed a series of tight maneuvers, weaving through a dense cluster of asteroids.

Finally, they emerged into a relatively clear space, where a lone, irregularly shaped asteroid hung suspended, its surface shimmering with an unnatural glow.

"Looks like it's playing host to some kind of energy field," Captain Reyes observed, her eyes narrowed in suspicion.

"Could be a trap."

Lyra studied the charts.

"There's no mention of an energy field on Aella's map. This might be Corvus' doing."

A tense silence filled the cockpit.

Was this a dead end, a carefully laid Corvus trap, or the actual location of the fragment?

They couldn't afford to waste time, but recklessly charging in was just as foolish.

"There's gotta be a way to bypass the field," Jax muttered, his cybernetic eye whirring as he scanned the asteroid's surface.

"Maybe a weak point..."

Suddenly, an alarm blared, red lights flashing on the console.

"Incoming fighters!"

Captain Reyes barked.

"Corvus must've tracked us."

Two sleek, black Corvus fighters emerged from behind a nearby asteroid, their laser cannons targeting The Discord.

Jax reacted instinctively, throwing the ship into a series of evasive maneuvers.

"We can't fight them head-on," Lyra shouted.

"We need to lose them in the asteroid field!"

A frantic chase ensued, the cramped cockpit filled with the roar of engines and the rhythmic staccato of laser fire.

Jax pushed The Discord to its limits, narrowly dodging laser blasts that scorched the asteroid's surface around them.

Just as it seemed like Corvus had them cornered, Captain Reyes spotted an opening – a narrow gap between two colossal asteroids.

"There!" she yelled. "Now!"

Jax, with a daring move, steered The Discord into the gap.

The Corvus fighters hesitated, their bulky frames unable to follow through the tight space.

Lyra watched in the rearview as the fighters shrunk, their frustrated laser fire glancing harmlessly off the asteroids.

"We lost them," Jax announced, a hint of triumph in his voice.

But the victory was short-lived.

"But we also lost our exit," Captain Reyes pointed out grimly.

They were trapped within the asteroid field, with no clear path back to the relative safety of Kepler-186f.

Lyra swallowed hard.

This wasn't just about retrieving the fragment anymore; it was about survival.

They were trapped, deep within the heart of the asteroid belt, with no way out and a powerful enemy on their tail.

The echoes of the past had led them to a dead end, and the symphony of defiance seemed to be playing a discordant note of despair.

Lyra slumped in her seat, the weight of their predicament crushing down on her.

Was this it?

Were they destined to become another casualty in Corvus' relentless pursuit of control?

But then, a flicker of defiance sparked within her.

They weren't done yet.

The symphony, even incomplete, held a power they hadn't fully explored.

Maybe, just maybe, it held the key to their escape.

"Captain," she said, her voice gaining strength, "remember the research station? The Harbinger? It could manipulate sound waves..."

Captain Reyes' eyes lit up with understanding.

"You're thinking what I'm thinking? We use the fragment, the asteroid field's natural resonance... maybe we can create a sonic disruption."

Jax, ever the pragmatist, chimed in.

"Risky, but it might work. The fragment could amplify the asteroid's natural frequencies, throw off Corvus' scanners, and even damage their ships."

Lyra reached into her pocket, her fingers brushing the worn leather case containing the fragment.

It wasn't just a piece of music anymore; it was a weapon, a desperate gamble against an overwhelming foe.

With a deep breath, she activated the case, the fragment within glowing with a pulsing light.

The cockpit filled with a strange melody, a haunting dissonance that resonated with the asteroid itself.

The ship vibrated around them, the air crackling with unseen energy.

Outside, the asteroid field seemed to come alive.

The rocks themselves vibrated, emitting a low, rhythmic hum that grew in intensity.

Lights on the Corvus fighters flickered erratically, their scanners emitting a cacophony of static.

Suddenly, with a deafening boom, one of the Corvus fighters exploded, its mangled remains tumbling towards an unsuspecting asteroid.

Fear and confusion rippled through the remaining fighter, its pilot desperately trying to regain control.

The sonic disruption intensified, the asteroid field erupting into a chaotic symphony of sound and fury.

Rocks shattered, sending debris flying in all directions.

The remaining Corvus fighter, caught in the crossfire, sputtered and died, its lifeless husk disappearing amidst the swirling chaos.

The cockpit lights dimmed, the fragment's glow fading as the last note of the discordant symphony faded away.

Silence descended, broken only by the ragged gasps of the crew, their ears ringing from the cacophony.

Lyra stared out the viewport, the wreckage of the Corvus fighters drifting amidst the asteroid field.

They had survived, against all odds.

The echoes of the past, though leading them into a trap, had also given them a weapon – a weapon not of violence, but of dissonance, a melody of rebellion that had disrupted their enemy's control.

Captain Reyes leaned back, a weary smile gracing her lips.

"Looks like the symphony just played a new movement, wouldn't you say, Lyra?"

Lyra nodded, a newfound determination burning in her eyes.

They had a long road ahead, filled with danger and uncertainty.

But they had tasted victory, however small.

The symphony of defiance, once a beacon of hope, now held the potential to become a weapon for liberation, not just a tool of manipulation.

With a renewed spirit, they set about navigating the treacherous asteroid field, searching for a way out.

The echoes of the past would continue to guide them, but now they were composing their own melody, a symphony of defiance that would resonate across the galaxy, challenging Corvus' control and inspiring a rebellion that would shake the very foundations of their oppressive regime.

Their journey had become a testament to the enduring power of music, its ability to unite, to inspire, and even to shatter the silence of oppression with a discordant roar.

The symphony of defiance had begun, and the galaxy was finally listening.

Chapter 17: Echoes of Discontent

The escape from the asteroid field proved just as harrowing as the chase itself.

Navigating the debris-laden labyrinth was a test of Jax's piloting skills and The Discord's battered hull.

Finally, after hours of weaving through a graveyard of asteroids, they found a navigable route leading back to the relative safety of deep space.

Exhaustion hung heavy in the air as they settled into a course back to Kepler-186f.

Lyra cradled the fragment, still faintly warm from its use.

The melody it held, a discordant dissonance, echoed in her mind, now laced with the satisfaction of their narrow escape.

"We did it," Captain Reyes finally spoke, her voice hoarse but filled with a quiet pride.

"We used the symphony against them. A weapon not of destruction, but of disruption."

Jax chuckled, a dry rasping sound.

"Yeah, a weapon that almost deafened us in the process."

Lyra smiled faintly.

"True, but it worked. And maybe that's what makes it powerful. Not brute force, but a way to sow confusion, to break through their control."

Her thoughts drifted back to Aella and the holographic projections depicting the symphony's history – a tool for unity turned into an instrument of division.

This wasn't just about regaining control of the symphony; it was about reclaiming its original purpose – a bridge between cultures, a melody that could resonate with every corner of the galaxy.

"We need to learn more about these fragments," she said, her voice gaining conviction.

"Each one holds a piece of history, a piece of the symphony's power. Understanding them might be the key to unlocking their true potential."

Captain Reyes nodded.

"Agreed. But where do we start? Aella's map only pointed to locations, not the nature of the fragments themselves."

Lyra glanced at the charts displayed on the salvaged tablet.

Each highlighted location seemed shrouded in mystery.

An abandoned temple on a gas giant, a lost colony ship drifting aimlessly, a desolate moon orbiting a decaying binary star system.

"Maybe the fragments hold clues within them," she suggested.

"Maybe each one contains a recording, a message from the past that could tell us about its purpose, its intended effect on the overall symphony."

Jax tapped his cybernetic eye thoughtfully.

"We might need to build an interface, a way to decode the data stored within the fragments. My engineering skills could come in handy here."

A glimmer of hope flickered within Lyra.

Even without knowing the full nature of their mission, they had a plan, a first step.

They were no longer simply rebels on the run; they were becoming researchers, and archaeologists of a forgotten art form, uncovering the secrets of a weaponized melody.

Days bled into weeks as they journeyed back to Kepler-186f.

Jax, fueled by coffee and an engineer's passion, tinkered away, piecing together a makeshift interface from salvaged components.

Lyra spent hours studying the fragment, searching for any hidden message, any flicker of a past voice.

Finally, just as they were nearing Kepler-186f, a breakthrough arrived.

Jax, with a triumphant grin, announced he'd managed to decipher a basic data stream from the fragment.

Hooking it up to the interface, a holographic image shimmered into existence.

It depicted a vast chamber filled with beings from different species, their skin tones, and features a kaleidoscope of alien beauty.

They stood, hands clasped, listening intently to an ethereal melody that resonated throughout the chamber.

A feeling of peace, of unity, emanated from the image.

Lyra felt a tear roll down her cheek.

This was what the symphony was meant for, not to control, but to connect.

A single image, a fragment of the past, had offered a glimpse of the symphony's true potential.

But the image flickered, and a new scene replaced it.

The same chamber, now filled with discord and struggle.

The melody warped, and twisted into a haunting cacophony that sent shivers down Lyra's spine.

The beings recoiled from each other, fear and suspicion etched on their faces.

The holographic projection faded, leaving the crew in a stunned silence.

The fragment, a single note in the grand symphony, held both the potential for unity and the seeds of its destruction.

Their mission, they realized with a growing sense of urgency, wasn't just about retrieving the remaining fragments; it was about rewriting the symphony's finale, turning a discordant melody into a call for liberation that would resonate across the galaxy.

As they touched down on Kepler-186f, a renewed determination burned within them.

They had a long road ahead, filled with danger and uncertainty.

Corvus wouldn't rest until they were silenced, their message of defiance crushed.

But with each recovered fragment, their understanding of the symphony grew.

Each note held a piece of history, a glimpse of the galaxy's diverse cultures and their responses to the music.

They discovered fragments on the gas giant, weathered recordings whispering of a forgotten paradise before the symphony's manipulation.

Deep in the wreckage of the lost colony ship, they found a fragment encoding a desperate plea for unity as resources dwindled and despair threatened.

On the desolate moon, a fragment showcased a vibrant festival, where the symphony, untainted, brought laughter and joy to a struggling community.

With each fragment, Jax's makeshift interface grew in complexity.

He deciphered not just music, but also data streams detailing the technical aspects of the symphony – its manipulation techniques, and the emotional triggers embedded within each note.

Lyra, analyzing both the fragments and historical records, began to theorize how to "recompose" the symphony, to rewrite its final act.

Their work attracted attention.

Rumors of a rebellion wielding a weaponized symphony spread through the galaxy like wildfire.

Whispers of hope reached oppressed planets, sparking pockets of resistance.

Corvus, desperate to snuff out this growing defiance, intensified their hunt for the rebels.

The pressure was immense.

Lyra, haunted by the symphony's history, felt the weight of responsibility on her shoulders.

One wrong note could sow further discord, and fracture the nascent rebellion before it truly began.

Jax, ever the pragmatist, kept them grounded, reminding them that any symphony, even a flawed one, was better than the oppressive silence of Corvus' regime.

Finally, after months of grueling work, they had it – a potential final movement for the symphony.

With a combination of salvaged technology, Jax's engineering genius, and Lyra's understanding of the past fragments, they created a new note – a beacon of hope, woven from the threads of the galaxy's diverse cultures and emotions.

But deploying it would be their greatest gamble.

They needed a platform, a way to broadcast their symphony across the stars. And they knew just where to find it.

Chapter 18: Echoes Across the Stars

THE COORDINATES, GLEANED from cryptic messages hidden within the fragments, pointed them towards a forgotten marvel – the abandoned orbital broadcast station, nestled in the rings of a gas giant named Hyperion.

Built millennia ago, it was rumored to be capable of transmitting across vast stretches of the galaxy.

Their journey was fraught with peril.

Corvus, having intercepted transmissions from Kepler-186f, had deployed a blockade around Hyperion.

Jax, piloting The Discord with his usual daredevil flair, used their knowledge of the asteroid field to weave through the Corvus fleet, evading laser fire and scrambling their scanners.

Finally, they breached the blockade and entered the swirling chaos of Hyperion's ring system.

There, amidst the glittering ice and swirling dust hung the colossal, skeletal frame of the orbital station.

It resembled a broken spiderweb, its once-powerful antennae dangling limply.

Landing on a precariously stable platform clinging to the station's outer hull, they found themselves staring into a vast, cavernous interior.

Dust motes danced in the pale light filtering through cracked panels, remnants of forgotten technology scattered across the floor.

"This place looks like it's been dead for centuries," muttered Jax, his cybernetic eye scanning the desolate environment.

Lyra, however, felt a flicker of hope.

If they could repair the broadcast station, and amplify its signal, they could unleash their recomposed symphony across the galaxy.

It would be a gamble, a defiant act that could unite the oppressed or draw Corvus' full wrath.

"Captain," called out Jax, his voice echoing in the vast chamber.

"Over here! Looks like a control center. Mostly intact."

Following Jax, they found a dusty control room, its holographic displays flickering erratically.

Years of neglect had taken their toll, but the core components seemed functional.

Jax, fueled by a surge of determination, rolled up his sleeves and began scanning the systems.

"This is gonna take some time," he announced after a cursory examination.

"Lots of repairs needed, and I'm no miracle worker."

Lyra understood.

They needed a distraction, a way to buy Jax some time to work his magic on the ancient technology.

A mischievous glint sparked in her eye.

"Captain," she said, a playful smile on her face, "remember that fragment we recovered from the Corvus fighter?"

Captain Reyes snorted.

"The one filled with their glorious propaganda? The one meant to inspire fear?"

"Exactly," Lyra continued, her voice filled with a dangerous glint.

"Let's turn their weapon against them. Let's give them a taste of their own medicine."

With a few deft modifications to their salvaged equipment, they managed to tap into the fragment.

Instead of the usual Corvus propaganda, they broadcasted a mocking message, a playful distortion of the original symphony.

A cacophony of discordant notes filled the airwaves, a satirical commentary on the regime's oppressive rule.

The effect was immediate.

Corvus ships, caught off guard by the unexpected broadcast, erupted in confusion.

Their internal comms went haywire, replaced by the mocking symphony.

Frustration and anger crackled through the blockade as their soldiers scrambled to regain control.

Inside the control room, Lyra and Captain Reyes watched in quiet amusement as the chaos unfolded on the holographic displays.

This was just a taste, a small act of rebellion that had sown discord within the enemy ranks. But it had also bought them precious time.

Jax, hammering away at the control panels, a sheen of sweat on his brow, finally turned to them.

"Alright, ladies," he announced, a hint of pride in his voice.

"She's ready to sing. But this is a one-shot deal. Once we activate the broadcast, there's no turning back."

Lyra took a deep breath, the weight of the galaxy on her shoulders.

This was it - the moment they had been working towards, the culmination of their desperate journey.

With a resolute nod, she met Captain Reyes' gaze.

"Then let's play."

Together, they activated the broadcast station.

A surge of energy pulsed through the skeletal structure, and the dormant antennae hummed back to life.

Lyra uploaded the recomposed final movement of the symphony, a melody woven from the hopes of countless oppressed worlds.

And then, the music washed out.

Across the galaxy, on every station not under Corvus control, the symphony began to play.

It was a melody of defiance, of unity, of a yearning for freedom.

The discordant notes resonated with the struggles of countless beings, a call to rise against their oppressors.

In Corvus headquarters, amidst the chaos of their disrupted communications, a single figure watched the symphony

Chapter 19: Echoes of Rebellion

IN THE OPULENT COMMAND center of Corvus headquarters, Chancellor Nero slammed his fist on the holographic display.

The distorted symphony blared, a mocking echo of his own propaganda, its defiance grating on his nerves.

He watched, enraged, as reports of unrest poured in from planets across the galaxy.

The rebels, these upstarts with their weaponized music, had thrown a wrench into his carefully constructed machine of control.

"Find them!" he roared, his voice echoing in the cavernous hall.

"Crush them before this... this... cacophony spreads further!"

His lieutenants scrambled, their faces etched with a mixture of fear and frustration.

The unexpected attack had caught them off guard, sowing discord within the ranks and stirring the embers of rebellion in long-subdued populations.

Meanwhile, aboard the orbital station, Lyra watched the galaxy react in real-time.

Images flickered across the holographic display – jubilant crowds on formerly oppressed planets, cheers erupting on spaceships, even hesitant defiance flickering in the eyes of Corvus soldiers.

The symphony, their defiant melody, was resonating.

"It's working," Captain Reyes breathed beside her, a flicker of hope dancing in her eyes.

Jax, ever the pragmatist, tempered their enthusiasm.

"Hold on. Corvus won't take this lying down. We've poked the hornet's nest. Expect retaliation, and soon."

His words were prophetic.

Suddenly, alarms blared, red lights flashing in the control room.

On the holographic display, a swarm of Corvus fighters emerged from the gas giant's shadow, converging on the orbital station.

"They've found us," Captain Reyes declared, her voice grim.

Lyra gritted her teeth.

They had achieved their objective, and broadcasted the symphony, but escape seemed unlikely.

This was their stand, their final act of defiance.

"Jax," Captain Reyes said, her voice filled with steely resolve, "get us out of here if you can. We can't let them capture the symphony."

Jax threw her a wry smile.

"Always thinking ahead, Captain. But let's not forget style points, shall we?"

He began a series of rapid-fire commands, rerouting power to the station's dormant defensive systems.

With a satisfying whirring, laser turrets emerged from hidden compartments, targeting the incoming Corvus fighters.

A fierce battle ensued.

The orbital station, a relic awakened from its slumber, roared to life.

Lasers ripped through the darkness, shields flared briefly before failing under the onslaught.

Corvus fighters fell, but more followed, their relentless assault threatening to overwhelm the station's defenses.

Lyra and Captain Reyes, wielding salvaged weapons, fought alongside the holographic projections of the symphony's creators – a motley crew of alien musicians from across the galaxy.

It was a symbolic fight, a testament to the unifying power of music, even in this moment of desperation.

But the battle was ultimately unsustainable.

The station, crippled by years of neglect, groaned under the attack.

A critical hit sent a tremor through the entire structure, and the holographic projections flickered and faded.

Just as it seemed all hope was lost, a new signal flickered on the holographic display.

It was a scrambled message, emanating from deep within Corvus headquarters.

A single word echoed amidst the static: "Defiance."

Lyra's eyes widened.

This wasn't a regular Corvus transmission.

This was someone inside, someone sympathetic to their cause, risking everything to send a message of support.

A flicker of hope rekindled in the control room.

They weren't alone.

The symphony, their defiant melody, had touched even the hearts of their enemies.

The battle raged on, but with renewed vigor.

The rebels, inspired by the unexpected message, fought with desperate ferocity.

The Corvus fighters, their attack faltering under the combined pressure, started breaking formation.

Suddenly, a new wave of ships emerged from the gas giant's shadow.

But these weren't Corvus fighters.

These were ships from various oppressed planets, responding to the symphony's call, and answering the plea for freedom.

The tide of the battle turned.

Corvus fighters were overwhelmed, retreating in chaos.

The orbital station, battered but not broken, held its stand as a symbol of defiance.

As the last Corvus ship disappeared into the void, Lyra collapsed onto the control panel, exhaustion washing over her.

They had survived, against all odds.

The symphony, their desperate gamble, had become a rallying cry for freedom.

But the fight was far from over.

News of their victory would spread, inspiring further rebellion.

Corvus, wounded but not defeated, would retaliate.

The galaxy held its breath as the Harbinger, the symbol of Corvus' power, hovered ominously above the orbital station.

The battle lines were drawn, not with lasers and missiles, but with the melody of defiance emanating from the station.

Lyra watched, her fingers clenched on the railing, as Commander Aric and his defectors engaged in a tense standoff with the remaining loyal Corvus forces.

Their act of rebellion, sparked by the symphony, threatened to crack open the very foundation of Corvus' regime.

But Chancellor Nero, a figure of pure rage on the Harbinger's bridge, wasn't one to give up easily.

He activated a massive device, dormant within the warship's hull.

A wave of static washed over the station, momentarily disrupting the symphony.

A holographic projection flickered into existence, revealing a twisted, nightmarish version of the symphony.

"This," Chancellor Nero's voice boomed across the comms, laced with a chilling calm, "is the true symphony. A weapon not of rebellion, but of control. A melody that will bend your minds to my will!"

Lyra felt a pang of fear.

They had underestimated Corvus.

This twisted symphony, a dark echo of the original, held an insidious power.

Disturbing images flashed across the holographic display – minds fracturing, wills weakening under the control of the corrupted melody.

Panic erupted among the crew.

Volunteers fumbled at their stations, their resolve momentarily wavering.

The defectors' ships wavered, their weapons pointed precariously between loyalists and the station.

Lyra knew they had to fight back, not just with weapons, but with their own music.

With trembling hands, she accessed the remaining fragments, searching for a melody strong enough to counter the Chancellor's insidious attack.

And then, she found it.

A fragment from a long-lost civilization, a melody pulsating with raw, untamed freedom. It wasn't perfect, but it held a primal power, a defiance that resonated at the very core of being.

"Play it!" she barked, her voice shaking with newfound determination.

The station's speakers roared to life, unleashing a torrent of raw, dissonant music.

It clashed with Chancellor Nero's warped melody, creating a cacophony that threatened to rip apart the fabric of space itself.

The battle between the melodies mirrored the battle raging between the ships.

Defectors, their resolve strengthened by the rebellious music, fought alongside the station's crew with renewed ferocity.

But the corrupted symphony was potent, its insidious tendrils reaching out, sowing confusion and doubt.

Suddenly, a tremor shook the station.

One of Corvus' warships, caught in the crossfire of the clashing melodies, exploded in a blinding flash.

The shockwave sent a wave of panic through both fleets

Lyra saw her opportunity.

Grabbing the microphone, she addressed the Corvus soldiers, her voice amplified across the chaotic battlefield.

"Soldiers! Don't be puppets to a tyrant's song! Listen to what's truly in your hearts! Fight for freedom, for your families, for a better future!"

Her words, echoing with the rebellious music, struck a chord.

Across the battlefield, Corvus soldiers hesitated, their faces contorted in internal struggle.

Was this the melody they truly served?

The first flicker of defiance spread like wildfire.

A Corvus fighter broke formation, its pilot joining the defectors.

Then another, and another.

The balance of power shifted, the tide turning against the Chancellor's loyal forces.

The climax was short-lived but brutal.

In a desperate attempt to regain control, Chancellor Nero unleashed the full power of his corrupted symphony.

The station shuddered, its systems overloading.

The crew screamed, clutching their heads as the dark melody infiltrated their minds.

Just as hope seemed lost, a wave of energy erupted from the defectors' ships.

They had reprogrammed their weapons, turning them into sonic amplifiers.

A concentrated blast of rebellious music, fueled by a galaxy yearning for freedom, slammed into the Harbinger.

A blinding light filled the void.

Then, silence.

The Harbinger, its control system overloaded, spiraled out of control, disappearing into the gas giant's atmosphere.

The battle was over.

Exhausted but exhilarated, the remaining ships gathered around the battered orbital station.

The air crackled with a sense of cautious optimism.

They had won a battle, but the war was far from over.

As Lyra surveyed the battlefield, the weight of the future settled on her shoulders.

They had a galaxy to awaken.

The news of their victory, fueled by the symphony's defiant melody, spread like wildfire across the stars.

Oppressed planets erupted in celebration, throwing off the yoke of Corvus control.

Resistance groups, once fragmented and fearful, united under the banner of the orbital station, their rebellion fueled by music.

Lyra, hailed as a symbol of hope, found herself thrust into a leadership role she never anticipated.

But looking at the faces of the newly liberated, the veterans hardened by years of oppression and the young yearning for a better future, she knew there was no turning back.

Their first task: securing the symphony.

Corvus wouldn't hesitate to develop their own weaponized melodies, twisting the original's power for even more sinister purposes.

Lyra, with a team of researchers, delved deeper into the fragments, deciphering not just musical notes, but the technology behind it.

They discovered the symphony wasn't just a series of melodies; it was a complex code, a language of emotions and actions.

By understanding its core structure, they could not only manipulate existing fragments but potentially compose entirely new ones – melodies tailored to specific situations, inspiring courage in times of battle, or fostering cooperation during reconstruction.

Meanwhile, Jax and his team of engineers worked tirelessly to repair the orbital station, transforming it into a beacon of hope, a central hub for the fledgling rebellion.

The once-abandoned platform became a bustling metropolis, filled with refugees, strategists, and musicians from across the galaxy.

Here, new melodies were born, each note a testament to the diverse cultures yearning for freedom.

But the fight was far from over.

Corvus, reeling from the unexpected rebellion, regrouped in the shadows.

Chancellor Nero, though wounded, wouldn't relinquish his grip on power easily.

Rumors reached the station of a secret weapon, a sonic dampener capable of silencing the symphony's influence.

The galaxy held its breath, waiting for the next act in this war fought through music.

Lyra, determined to protect their weapon and their fledgling rebellion, knew they needed to be proactive.

They had to find and neutralize the Corvus weapon before it silenced the burgeoning revolution.

Thus began their next chapter: a daring mission into the heart of Corvus territory, a quest to unravel the secrets of the sonic dampener and ensure the symphony's message of liberation continued to resonate across the stars.

Their journey would be fraught with danger, forcing them to confront not just Corvus forces, but also the darker aspects of their own weaponized music.

For in the fight for freedom, even the most noble melodies had a price.

Chapter 20: Whispers in the Dark

WEEKS BLED INTO MONTHS as the orbital station, now christened "Harmonia," buzzed with activity.

Refugees from liberated planets mingled with veteran rebels, their collective energy fueling the rebellion's fledgling flame.

Lyra, burdened by the mantle of leadership, spent her days deciphering the symphony's secrets, her nights haunted by nightmares of Chancellor Nero's twisted melodies.

News arrived daily, a cacophony of hope and despair.

Freed planets struggled to rebuild, while Corvus forces, though weakened, retaliated with brutal crackdowns.

The galaxy remained a patchwork of liberation and oppression, a testament to the symphony's power as both a rallying cry and a tactical weapon.

One evening, as Lyra pored over a salvaged Corvus data pad, a shadow fell across her desk.

Captain Reyes, her face etched with worry, stood before her.

"We intercepted a coded transmission," she said, her voice grim.

"It originates from deep within Corvus territory, a location matching rumors of their sonic dampener project."

Lyra's heart pounded.

A silent symphony – a weapon capable of negating their greatest advantage.

"We can't let them deploy it," she declared, her voice tight with determination.

"We agree," said Captain Reyes.

"But a frontal assault is suicide. We need a small, covert team to infiltrate the facility, disable the dampener, and retrieve any relevant data."

Lyra's gaze swept across the bustling station.

Doctors treating the wounded, engineers tinkering with salvaged technology, musicians collaborating on new melodies – none of them suited for clandestine missions.

Except for one.

"Jax," she murmured, the name heavy with a mix of hope and trepidation.

Jax, ever the tinkerer, stood amidst a pile of salvaged weaponry, his hands ghosting over a disassembled Corvus fighter drone.

He looked up, his single cybernetic eye flickering with curiosity as Lyra and Captain Reyes approached.

"Going on a little recon mission, are we?" he quipped, a hint of a smirk playing on his lips.

"More like a suicide mission," Captain Reyes corrected bluntly.

Jax's smile faltered.

"What's the target?"

Lyra explained about the sonic dampener and the potential threat it posed to their entire resistance.

By the end of her explanation, Jax's face was a mask of seriousness.

"Alright," he conceded, rubbing his jaw with a grease-stained hand.

"But I won't do it alone. I need someone who knows Corvus tech inside and out."

His gaze settled on a figure across the room – a young woman, a former Corvus engineer who had defected during the battle of Hyperion.

She returned his stare, a mix of fear and defiance in her eyes.

"Riya," Jax said, his voice gentle, "we need your help."

Riya hesitated for a moment, then squared her shoulders.

"I owed a debt to the old regime," she said, her voice firm.

"Now, I owe one to freedom."

Lyra watched a flicker of hope rekindle in Jax's eye.

A small team, a high-risk operation – the perfect recipe for a disaster, or perhaps, a turning point in the fight for liberation.

Days flew by in a flurry of planning. Jax, with Riya's help, modified a captured Corvus drone, cloaking it with technology scavenged from the Harbinger.

They would infiltrate the facility disguised as a Corvus patrol, relying on Riya's knowledge of the base layout and her ability to bypass security protocols.

The night before the mission, Lyra stood by the docking bay, watching Jax and Riya disappear into the cockpit of the modified drone.

A knot of worry tightened in her stomach.

These were her friends, her comrades in arms, and now, they were venturing into the heart of the enemy's territory.

"May the harmony be with you," she murmured, a phrase that had become their unofficial motto.

The drone launched into the void, a silent speck disappearing into the vastness of space.

Back in the heart of Harmonia, the symphony continued to play, its defiant melody a testament to their fight.

But the silence of the departing drone hung heavy in the air, a chilling reminder of the perilous journey that lay ahead for Jax and Riya.

Don't miss out!

Visit the website below and you can sign up to receive emails whenever Marquise The Coach publishes a new book. There's no charge and no obligation.

https://books2read.com/r/B-A-QBWDB-GKQDD

BOOKS 2 READ

Connecting independent readers to independent writers.

About the Author

As an author, coach, and advocate for holistic living, Marquise is on a mission to change lives—one mindset at a time. With a passion for inspiring mindfulness, awareness, and sustainable living, Marquise's journey is deeply rooted in a commitment to personal growth and societal well-being.

From a young age, Marquise felt called to make a positive impact on the world, driven by a profound sense of empathy and compassion for others. This innate desire led Marquise to pursue a path dedicated to understanding the complexities of the human mind and exploring innovative approaches to fostering well-being.

With years of experience as a coach and mentor, Marquise has witnessed firsthand the transformative power of mindfulness and awareness. By guiding individuals to cultivate a deeper connection with themselves and the world around them, Marquise empowers others to live authentically and consciously, making choices aligned with their values and aspirations.

In addition to promoting personal growth, Marquise is deeply passionate about sustainable living and environmental stewardship.

Recognizing the interconnectedness of all living beings and the planet we call home, Marquise advocates for mindful consumption, eco-friendly practices, and conscious living habits that honor the Earth and support future generations.

Through Marquise's writing, coaching, and advocacy efforts, countless individuals have found inspiration, guidance, and empowerment on their journey toward a more fulfilling and sustainable way of life. With unwavering dedication and a heart full of compassion, Marquise continues to make a difference in the world, one mindset at a time.

Read more at https://marquisethecoach.com/.